Quick Rick

3

Rick bumps into Tom and his little, brown dog, Fuzz.

I am so quick. I am quicker than a car!

Rick and Tom do not see Bad Val.
Bad Val grabs Fuzz!

Rick is quick. He will get Bad Val.

Rick bursts in. He turns off the jet.

Splutter! Splutter!

Bad Val can not get out.

Rick has got Fuzz and Bad Val.

You are too quick for me!

Ruff! Ruff!